I AM FAMOUS

by Tara Luebbe and Becky Cattie

pictures by Joanne Lew-Vriethoff

Albert Whitman & Company
Chicago, Illinois

To Derick W. and Becky S.—my literary glam squad—TL

For Hannah, my favorite diva—BC

To Maarten with love—JLV

Library of Congress Cataloging-in-Publication data is on file with the publisher.

Text copyright © 2018 by Tara Luebbe and Becky Cattie

Pictures copyright © 2018 by Joanne Lew-Vriethoff

Published in 2018 by Albert Whitman & Company

ISBN 978-0-8075-3440-3

Printed in China

10 9 8 7 6 5 4 3 2 1 WKT 22 21 20 19 18 17

Design by Jordan Kost

For more information about Albert Whitman & Company,
visit our website at www.albertwhitman.com.

I am famous.

I am an actress,

a singer,

and a dancer.

Daddy says I'm also a diva...
whatever that is.

I've been famous for as long as I can remember.

A Star Is Born

It was obvious early on
that I had special talents,

a unique style,

and a flair for
the dramatic.

Because I am famous,
I get special treatment
wherever I go.

I have my own chef, driver, and housekeeper.

My fan club spoils me.

All my movies go viral.

46

436 views • 18 likes

The paparazzi follow me everywhere. In showbiz, that means photographers who take pictures of famous people, like me.

Sometimes it's annoying.

They bother me when I'm dining.

They chase me while I'm driving.

They invade my privacy!
"Do something cute," they beg.
Oh, the price of fame!

Tonight I'm performing at Grandpa's birthday party.
This will be my biggest show yet.

My stylist arrives.
We discuss the right look.

I hit the red carpet.

Wait! I need my sunglasses.
Famous people *always*
wear sunglasses.
"Break a leg!" Daddy says.
In showbiz, that means
good luck.

It's a packed house.

I've never seen so many fans.

Showtime!

For act one,
I sing Grandpa's
favorite song.

Uh-oh! What were
the words again?
Just keep smiling.
The show must go on!
La la la...

Intermission.

Now for act two...

I dazzle them with my latest dance moves.
Ouch! Just keep smiling. The show *must* go on!

And the grand finale...

How humiliating! I'll never work in this town again.

What's happening? Is that applause?
It's my fans!

They still love me, no matter what.
And that's the *best* part about being a star.

I am still famous.